Silhouette in the Sunset

One Hundred Poems on the Futility of War

by

Colin Ward

In
As Many
WORDS

Published by *In As Many Words*

www.inasmanywords.com

ISBN 978-1-9998089-4-5
Paperback

Cover & book design by Colin Ward
Cover painting *"The Futility of War"* by Rob Parkinson

First printed June 2019

For Mum.
Love always.

"If you could hear, at every jolt, the blood
Come gargling from the froth-corrupted lungs,
Obscene as cancer, bitter as the cud
Of vile, incurable sores on innocent tongues,—
My friend, you would not tell with such high zest
To children ardent for some desperate glory,
The old Lie: *Dulce et decorum est*
Pro patria mori."

Wilfred Owen
From "Dulce et Decorum Est"

Contents

Introduction..i

One Hundred Years................................1

We Honour the Brave 2

What Our Fathers Were Fighting For 3

Brutal War..4

Brother's Bloody Story 4

Thou Shalt Not Kill 5

Good Meets Evil 5

Dear Mr Anderson..............................6

Hate...7

Slithering Honour..............................7

Old Foes.......................................7

Spitfire 7

Murder His Goodbye 8

Loss...9

Lonely Soldier 9

Summer's War..................................10

How Can I Thank You?.........................11

Old Secrets..................................12

Blade 13

Ashes...14

Born into War................................14

Call Me a Hero...............................15

Buried 15

Forgotten 16

Lord's Prayer................................18

Hate Calls...18

Play-Time Prisoner...19

Empty Sorrow...19

Sniper's Luck..20

War Dog..20

Tank-A..20

Machine Gun Man..21

I Don't Come to the Door No More........................22

Left Right..23

Peace Murdered..24

Questions..24

Loft-Whopper...25

My Hero..26

Call a Spade a Spade..26

Blitz & Thunderclap..27

Dog Fight..27

Children Playing...28

Insane..29

Can't Catch Me..30

Lonely Old Soldier...31

Song for the Fallen...32

Bear...32

Only Mothers Know..33

The Samurai..33

Crimson Liqueur...33

Silhouette in the Sunset...34

OTT...36

Nature's War...36

Beating Drum...37

Art of War..37

Mad Minute 37

Greatness 38

Patriot's Pledge 39

Mercenary Medals...39

Willow..40

Propaganda 40

Duty 40

Charge..41

Never Dare Ask Why 41

My Blood 42

Remember Hope 43

Banshee 43

Honour Them..44

Weapons..44

Soldier's Eulogy 45

Seasons of War..46

Valentine for Dresden 47

Chance of War 47

Peace...47

Shell Shock..48

PTSD 49

War Blunder 49

Who am I now? 50

Debt Across the Ages...51

Means & Ends...51

The Last Refuge...52

Sky Beasts 53

Sniper...53

Final Moment...54

Soldier's Goodbye...56

Shell...57

Dresden's Valentine 58

Last Supper..58

Birds of Britain...59

Pride in War...59

My Duty 60

Blackened..61

Brave 62

Secret Books of Auschwitz..............................63

Forgive..64

Bullet..65

Wealth...65

Ceasefire..65

Mr Anderson..66

A Letter Home..67

Acknowledgements...73

Other Works by the Author..............................75

Introduction

Silhouette in the Sunset has been created in tribute to the 100th year anniversary of the end of World War One. It is an unashamed pacifist voice throughout, written from a philosophical, social, political, and personal perspective.

I have arranged the collection in a relaxed order rather than grouping or categorising the poems thematically. Many ideas and thoughts are visited repeatedly, shaped in different ways, and shared through the voices of characters who speak the words. Dipping into the book to capture thoughts and ideas should be as fruitful as reading from cover-to-cover.

The collection is my exploration of many aspects of war, and what moves me most in the works of our greatest poets, such as Wilfred Owen, Rudyard Kipling, Siegfried Sassoon, to name but a few. Owen has always been one of my greatest inspirations and his work influenced me throughout this project. His brutal honesty is moving and emotive, laying bare the horrors of war that soldiers faced.

I hope to have captured a range of expression through rhythm, form, language and imagery, raising more questions than ever attempting to offer answers or solutions. Perhaps one major theme is how it seems increasingly difficult in this morally fractured world to truly differentiate between friend and foe.

One Hundred Years

Shed all the tears for one-hundred more years,
but our compass is now moral-rotten.
How dare we proclaim each year just the same
when each war says we've all long forgotten?

We Honour the Brave

Hold my hand
as I bow my head,
I do not understand
the tears I shed.

They are not for your courage,
your honour, or name,
the warmth of your memory,
my comfort all the same.

But each year passing,
the promise grows older,
our share of the grip
weakens ever colder.

We owe this lifetime's debt,
a century of Novembers,
words saying we never forget,
actions showing we fail to remember:

if future souls
are to be saved,
it can only be in peace
we truly honour the brave.

What Our Fathers Were Fighting For

When wars have yet to wish for an end,
profit is power, perfect to defend,
shared between the silver-tongued few
born blue with pride, but never grew,
demanding service to appreciate
gilded self-worthy golden gate,
forced-shut on faces of the poor:
is this what our fathers were fighting for?

When children must live longing for homes,
thousands suffer filthy streets they roam,
food demoted to a weapon of state,
dignity left dying from doomed debate,
humanity hidden to force our surrender,
justice reserved for the privileged offender,
this damn-nation gutter-shames its poor:
is this what our fathers were honoured for?

When hearts are strongest cold-stone-carved,
conscience left waning empathy-starved,
kindness, once kindred, fades to the past
since killing became the commodity to last,
guilt is a fault felt only by each other
so we can swim free in the blood of our brothers,
tears, falling dry, salt the wounds of the poor:
is this what our fathers were dying for?

Brutal War

Shoot,
be shot,
it's a choice,
we're not just boys
playing games on the playground anymore,
now we're men trading flesh in bloody war,
with vicious toys,
no more voice,
just hot
brute.

Brother's Bloody Story

We are brothers
shoulder to shoulder,
alone amongst others,

together we stand,
Over the Top we go
to no-man's land,

tagged like dogs,
tin-to-toe mud-matched
with minds of logs

to seek glory
for life's worth,
this bloody story.

Thou Shalt Not Kill

Thou shalt not kill,
so the commandment goes,
enshrined in our law,
set down so long ago,
by those far wiser,
guided directly by God:
murder, illegal,
unless a deity gives the nod.
Disguise yourself as nature,
decorate salutes with eagles,
only attack the enemy
when duty-blessed so regal,
who alleviate conscience
so you need not understand
anything about your foe
but that they live on oil-rich land.

Good Meets Evil

Stock shouldered by hate,
locked sights aiming at fate.
Rounds loaded to fire,
cut flesh like razor wire.
Peace silenced by years,
ceases for no man's tears.
Blood spilt by the lies,
good meets evil to die.

Dear Mr Anderson

Dear Mr Anderson,
shelter me again:
night has come,
sky is falling,
crying metal rain.

Please, Mr Anderson
dig me safely deep:
close my eyes,
hold my hand,
be my one-eyed sleep.

Why, Mr Anderson
must we hide away?
I can shoot,
fly a plane,
just a game we play.

Dear Mr Anderson,
why do they attack?
I'd ask my mum
but she went out,
don't know if she'll be back.

Hate

Hell has its own gate:
mankind's wrath and blind fury
open it with hate.

Slithering Honour

Slithering honour,
like Cleopatra's snakebite.
Pin Medals to breasts.

Old Foes

Old foes die harder,
innocence dies easily,
new friends live longest.

Spitfire

Heroes of our skies,
dancing their glorious glide,
saved freedom with pride.

Murder His Goodbye

Sudden crack
attacks the nerves,
betrays the delicate sentiment
of silent and sombre air
hanging heavy over ceremony
dressed too much
in pomp and circumstance.

Second jolt
rattles the bones,
disobeys the reflection
of memories earned
before violence took him,
torn from us,
serving supposed greater purpose.

Third snap
grips the neck,
choking the peace:
this is how he died,
life without celebration,
ended too soon,
and now

you murder his goodbye.

Loss

No battle is won
until one side counts the loss:
Nature weeps for all.

Lonely Soldier

Time came to leave,
no voice to my name,
to proud and prematurely,
celebrate my fame,
no bitter tears spread,
cursing my forsake,
fearing of foretelling
an honoured mistake.

Silence spoke as I marched,
with solemn intent,
committed civil service
like selling a morose circus,
no father's words of advice,
nor motherly tears of regret,
sister's trembling embrace,
or brother's wet-eyed forget.

Time came to leave
what I was fighting for:
nothing.

Summer's War

Today my battle
is with her blazing rays,
which dry the blood-rubble
as my mind is enslaved,
its own weary chief,
thirsty to remember
time long passed,
when summer's arms
were a welcome embrace.

Days of joyous bounty,
fruits of the harvest a plenty,
fields paved in lush-green-gold,
spread and rolled
across hilltops and valley drops,
a world as bright
as the future I'd see.

Close my eyes,
let her warm my memory,
running in fields
where young love bloomed
and burned in secret shades,
eternal promises made,
sealed with delicate daisies
laced in lucid gestures
of desire.

But not here, now,
as shadows curtain the sky,
land torn coarse and jagged,
ashed with flesh and bone,
hills chewed,
scattered with brass
splintered by carcassed
tools of death,
all the abuses mankind
delivers to itself.

How Can I Thank You?

How can I thank you,
though I should,
if only in evil
you fought for good?

My heart should honour
service and duty,
but dark purpose
shadowed your beauty.

I try to remember
sacrificed lives,
but how can death
be why hope survives?

Old Secrets

Dirt falling by my ears,
neck strains to gain
a glimpse of no-man's land.
My duty and mission
fill me with lead,
threaten to spill
cowardly into my under-carriage.
Courage whimpers my hands
over the edge of darkness,
pulling me into the abyss,
onto uneven ground
dashed with debris,
solid here, sinking there,
secrets of sullied air.
Nervous hands land
on a small metal dome,
distressed by divots,
ravaged by roughness,
battlefield bent,
cloaked under years of filth,
hidden up here,
in Great-Grandad's attic.
This old helmet,
proud of its history,
twice saving his life,
is heavy with his story,
which never passed lips
but for rambling,

whirlwinds of madness,
untold to generations.
This cold old helmet
saved his head
but not his mind,
spared his life,
but spurned his future.
I replace it,
leaving old secrets
to lie
alone.

Blade

Draw the Butcher's blade,
bloody serenade,
youthful splendour spills
final taste of kills,
covering defeat,
spreading Mother's peat,
factory of fear
mocked with misspent tears.

Forget the bloom of sorrow flower,
future fails to yield to its power.

Ashes

Honour my ashes
over rolling hills of life,
not fields where I fell.

Born into War

They were born with rattles
of the floor and doors,
first cries to crashing of steel;
their ears burned from screaming
at the turbulence of war
before they could know what was real.

First steps were practice
of the run for their lives,
feet blistered to the bone;
all the bullets and blasts,
only luck can survive,
if that's what you call life alone.

Youth-lost minds terror-filled,
forced to flee from their home,
like birds of the forest fires,
scorched and clipped wings
fail to land where they roam,
betrayed by compassion of liars.

Call Me a Hero

I kill a man with a knife
in the dead of night:
call me a murderer.

I kill a man with my fist
in a drunken fight:
call it manslaughter.

I kill a man with my rifle,
caught in my sight:
call me a hero.

Congratulate yourself
from your moral height:
because you call it war.

Buried

Have me buried next to my father,
my sons buried next to me,
if ever you learn war won't set us free,
we'll give you back your cemetery.

Forgotten

Do I taint your gracious path,
scarring gentrified surroundings,
polluting pomp,
prevent your serviced circumstance
upon honour
amongst thieves of future,
protected by my comrades?

Do my ramblings distract
your silenced woe,
my stench offending
finest senses of land
I spilt blood to protect,
whilst slings and arrows
narrow my nightmares,
righteous blank cannon
terrors my mind,
blasting shock memories
waking me each night,
driving me from my home?

Worry not,
I stand aside,
dismissed from ceremony,
forego your pride,
regret my misplaced matrimony,
displaced paternity,
shed my tears,
suffer my fears,
different doorway tonight.

Perhaps my last breath
as the living are honoured,
dead remembered,
those between
left,
bereft,
forgotten.

Lord's Prayer

I pray to you, my Lord,
today you might find
some other sorrowed soul,
body bloodied
and bereft, rotting broken
in the ground,
shattered by your abandon,
deafened with brutal
sound, as you sit listening
in wait for prayers
begging your throne to spare
our brothers' pain before leaving
them to die alone.

Hate Calls

Hush,
all walls
listening,
your betrayal,
delivered by your once innocent child,
no longer playing games, joyfully wild,
gives portrayal:
deafening
hate-calls
crush.

Play-Time Prisoner

We've catched us a prisoner,
best we've ever got!
He was trying to escape,
now he's stuck right on the spot
where I tied him up with rope,
me mate took off his shoes
so 'e aint going nowhere
or 'e'll be black 'n' blue.

Maybe we should shoot him,
bang, right in the 'ed
but he might be a crafty spy
and ain't no use if 'e is dead.
Mam says we should hurt 'em bad,
never ever let 'em go,
but bleed 'em bloody Jerries dry,
teach 'em hell like daddy knows.

Empty Sorrow

I shall not patronise you
with an empty platitude of sorrow
when I bring to your door
a message to declare
your son will never return
on any tomorrow.

Sniper's Luck

Once there was an arrogant sniper,
who thought he shot as sharp as a viper,
kept a tally of kills,
called them his thrills,
took great pleasure for stinging a striper.

But one night he ran out of luck,
boasting of a target he'd struck,
he let out a cheer,
making himself clear,
but should have been faster to duck.

War Dog

Train this weary dog
muzzle-stopped until battle
then command my bite.

Tank-A

Obese morbid slide
slowly tormenting the landscape
rusting with murder
snarls like a blood-thirsty bear
warlord petrifies its prey.

Machine Gun Man

Rattatat, rattatat
Machine Gun Man,
legs up, head down,
run as fast as I can.

Rattatat, rattatat
automatic enemy,
in their sights, taking aim,
they won't catch me.

Rattatat, rattatat
eating chains of rounds,
through the smoke, I approach,
slowly making ground.

Rattatat, rattatat
sweep the field with shells
heavy steps weigh me down
as I wade through bloody hell.

Ratta' –
all is quiet,
darker,
colder,
still.

I Don't Come to the Door No More

I don't come to the door no more,
don't see no point.
Ain't gonna be no little feet
come patterin
nor chitter no sweet chatterin,
or spillin them tears,
only Momma's sweet tea,
gentle kiss on a grazed knee,
can solve and bliss.
Won't be no more
clothes disgraced,
shoes unlaced
from wild boys chase,
runnin free.

I don't come to the door no more,
not since them uniforms came knockin.
Stood somber like news shockin
them souls,
look so solemn
sadness them don't own,
deliver on my doorstep
words to crash down my home.
I say they take my boy,
abuse him,
use him,
lose him,
leave me a folded flag.

No, I don't come to the door no more.
'Cause there ain't no-one to open it for.

Left Right

Left
right
left
right
left home
right dream
left in service
right for your pride
left in duty: king and country
right for honour: fight for future
left a loved one: home is waiting
right to die for: hero's return
left lost comrades
right for medals
left hope
right here
left
right
left
right.

Peace Murdered

Round chambered
stock shouldered
target acquired
sight aimed
trigger pulled
kill achieved
tally recorded
glory claimed
honour awarded
bravery celebrated.
Peace: murdered.

Questions

Never rely on
faith which demands obeying
truth that requires conveying
proof only heard when telling
stories too committed to selling
judgement built on hypocrisy
under cover of law and democracy
fuelled by the promises of liars
throwing your future onto fires:
because if war is the only suggestion,
we're still not asking the right questions.

Loft-Whopper

Out in the hallway
spinning the top
faster and faster,
all the world stops,
looks up to the sky,
shoulders all drop
to loud distant moaning,
warning and droning.

Gathered by Mother's arms,
sister clutched my hand,
all practised for alarm,
no time to understand,
just hide under stairs
as always planned,
out goes the last light
darker every night.

Grandfather swings,
creaking and clicking,
watching the house,
protecting with ticking,
wait for Loft-Whoppers,
'cause they'll come kicking,
knocking your door
and burying your floor.

My Hero

How can I call you my hero
when I despise your deeds?
Will duty bear the fruit of respect
if that's what courage needs?

Are we confusing necessity
with being morally free?
How much is one man's blood worth
to drop his foes to their knees?

Who declares our hearts must ache
so the powerful can be appeased?
Should we spill our souls in silence
but never muddy their memory?

Does honour really need a killing
when you're not fighting for me?

Call a Spade a Spade

Call a spade a spade,
marker where my body's laid,
hardly a well-made cenotaph,
adorned with first-grade epitaph,
dressed each year in floral sorrow,
honour begets the self-assuring borrow
of my name to fuel the fires
which power the machine of national liars.

Blitz & Thunderclap

Whistle down
deafening crash
swallow sound
fiery fangs
burn roofs
gobble walls
crumble homes
cities fall
ground quakes
nights awake
painful screams
filling dreams
same trap:
Blitz & Thunderclap.

Dog Fight

d-d-d-d-death defying
d-d-d-d-dancing flying
d-d-d-d-dogs attacking in the night

d-d-d-d-daring doubles
d-d-d-d-dad's in trouble
d-d-d-d-deadly dodgems of the flight

d-d-d-d-darkness hiding
d-d-d-d-doom-filled gliding
d-d-d-d-don't get caught in Jerry's sights.

Children Playing

I sit here watching
children playing,

running, arms splayed out,
soaring, spitting attacks,
they roll and tumble joyful shouts.
I wonder:
should I tell them about
fathers, brothers, sons,
heroes fighting
with the same machine-guns,
speaking different languages,
but not for fun?

Why spoil the beautiful mind,
born so wide-eyes-open,
unscarred and naturally kind
until the world darkens,
and innocence gets left behind?

Why plague their youth-warm dreams
by dragging cold night-time fears
into the comforting escape of day,
extend shadow-terrified tears,
and darkly cast hope away,
poisoned by lost years?

I sit here watching
children playing,

whilst the wretched truth
salts my cheeks,
bitter with knowledge,
their game may soon be over,
but will never be won.

Insane

I doubt my heart
can still love
or ever love again;
my faith is blind
to future's path
for anything but pain.

Lies are told,
hate is fuelled,
survive and don't be slain
fighting battles
for other men
discarded by disdain.

Keep your colours
and malice medals
soaked in bloody rain,
souls sacrificed
to win the human race
by driving it insane.

Can't Catch Me

You can't catch me,
king of hide and seek,
I see your SS boots
through slithered floorboard peeks.

No, you can't catch me,
'cause I hold my nose
from the choking dusty air,
and your stinking soldier toes.

So, you can't catch me,
I'm gonna make my run,
you think you have me cornered,
but I'm not afraid of Nazi guns.

Still, you can't catch me,
like you took my friends,
I'm not scared of you at all
'cause I know how this ends.

You can't catch me,
I'm not really here,
You've already claimed my bones,
I've nothing left to fear.

Lonely Old Soldier

His heart was right,
though dark at night,
by day felt heavily broken.

Ice on a lake,
summer's mistake,
mystery unspoken.

With truth too feared,
bludgeoned and speared,
chilling abyss held under.

His steps forbid
the boatman's rid,
'til Nature screams her thunder.

Vengeful descent
raining cement,
the cracking, hallowed ice-sheet.

Shoulders of lead,
drag down with dread,
betrayed by his own high-street.

Song for the Fallen

Sing a song
for the fallen fellow man,
bless his soul
for the lives he saved,
hold a moment of silence
for what we have lost,
in the honour
and duty he gave.

Rest your hand
on the stone in his memory,
run your fingers
through the gold of his name,
curse his story
for ending too soon,
but remember his love
was not to blame.

Bear

Roaring, clawing,
gnawing at the ground,
chewing through undergrowth,
screeching steel sounds,
tracking, attacking,
tearing down, trees,
rumble heavy tumbling,
metal menacing disease.

32

Only Mothers Know

Sing
like your boys are coming home;
dream
like you'll hear their voice again;
smile
like your heart has always known;
cry
like only mothers know the pain.

The Samurai

Gripped tight to the hilt,
feared art of a master,
honour sings the fine tune,
crafting slices of air,
single savage vicious roar
severs the crane's neck,
releasing butterfly's beauty
as life perishes.

Crimson Liqueur

Life's crimson liqueur
toasts raised by the flavoured few
drunk on death's glory.

Silhouette in the Sunset

Lying, battle-broken, sinking
into savaged terrain, disfigured
from the detritus
of war, cratered
as a mother's heart bleeds
with unnatural loss.

My eyes fight
the lead weight
of final sleep.

Sky burns in blasphemous beauty
as Hades' outstretched hand
claws for souls left behind.

Choked vision betrays my view
of a figure, seized by slanders of fatigue,
standing in sombre regret,
before a meagre monument
to a fallen comrade, lost greasing
the machine of combat
with his own blood.

I cannot identify his profile,
this hieroglyph etched
into the fiery backdrop, captured
by the cruel cadence of battle,
in familiar forlorn posture:
is he friend or foe?

Too weak to call out, I yield
my final sigh: it matters
not whose colour
my fellow wears,
when all are dead
and buried,
futility of war
has conquered,

I do not fear that none
shall remember,
but dread
that too many
will choose to forget

the sacrifice and secret solitude
of the silhouette in the sunset.

OTT

Battery rattles around
my head full of metal sound,
exploding shattered ears,
choking the mind with fear.

Cold shiver shocks
soaking in soiled socks
and blister-bitten boots,
up the burning shoots.

Final command - show my head
or else be chasten-dead,
so I clamber-climb free
to live and die by OTT.

Nature's War

She,
our home,
we abuse,
punish with fire,
tearing her skin with petty battling
collateral damages betraying
life we admire
as we choose
to roam
free.

Beating Drum

Beating on death's drum,
thrash rhythm calls end of time,
heart stops Nature's crime.

Art of War

When romancing the art of war,
brush-stroking the moral whore,
you can try to be saints
of the shade of your paint,
but blood is always red in the corps.

Mad Minute

Sixty-seconds of frenzied wrath
fighting war like psychopaths.

Reload, aim, and fire at speed,
fodder with machine-like greed.

Fingers cold, numbed down to bone,
but never stop, you're all alone.

Aim sights high, between the eyes,
then your soul won't hear the cries.

Greatness

Greatness for one,
salty righteousness
bitter on the tongue,
acrid taste of victory
spoils before long,
till sweet memories
make it soft,
dreams run like honey
holding hope aloft
until all freedom
has been scoffed,
chewed and spewed,
spat out vile
oily mess drooling
puddle-pooling bile,
sulphuric hot
steaming a while,
retching at the stink
we prefer to forget,
swallowing the cordite
flavour of regret,
hidden beneath
sombre fragrant rosettes
placed in honour.

Patriot's Pledge

The Patriot's pledge…
hand to heart,
faith to a God whose love,
malice-minded and brutality-bent,
demands that life be misspent,
sacrificed blindly by believing
murder is not merely cowardice,
camouflaged as valour,
until captured by madness,
arms risen to shield from nothing
tortured melted minds,
endlessly tormented by terror,
being abandoned by the social sewer,
which it needs to justify
faith to a God whose love,
hand to heart,
the Patriot's pledge…

Mercenary Medals

Take blood, bone, body,
but never forsake the soul,
nor spoil the spirit:
mercenary reptile tears,
can't buy mirth with medalled years.

Willow

Weep, Willow, weep,
let down your arms,
slip soft to sleep,
gliding to the ground
as your trunk crumbles
whisper those final sounds,
a last wistful breath
as you lay by your roots,
returning to the dust
from where you once grew.

Propaganda

Sticks and stones may break your bones
but hatred is what kills you.
Don't believe those righteous tones
just fickle lies to mock truth.

Duty

Duty demanded,
thunderstorm obedience,
leafed in uniform,
wrapped in her identity
to sully Mother's regret.

Charge

Take a horse, a sword and a shield,
charge the whole length of a field,
dive right into the clash
with a maniacal thrash,
and pray that the other sod yields.

Never Dare Ask Why

I'm tired of the telly-stations
telling me who is next to die,
thrusting thoughts of devastation,
celebrities who crocodile-cry:
"take the blame or make donations,"
and never dare ask why.

We're trapped in moral constipation,
forget the foreigners left to fry,
they only serve media manipulation,
man-made manuscripts of lies
to feed our feared imagination,
and never dare ask why.

We've sold the power of conversation,
punished when we dare to try
anti-social communication,
designed to suck our souls dry,
sapped by years of repatriation
and never dare ask why.

41

My Blood

Beating.
Flowing steady:
thankful of waking;
bitter of where.

Pounding.
Pumping treacle:
Ground is shaking;
hiding, too scared.

Racing.
Fluid rushing:
body is flying;
mind unprepared.

Thump.
Slowing thickness:
river drying;
numbing, and scared.

Shh.
Draining away:
soul escaping;
no more nightmares.

Remember Hope

Remember the darkest hours
when souls are viciously soured,
honour gets mistaken
as homes are forsaken
and dreams are bitterly devoured.

Victors are valiantly claimed
by millions murdered and maimed,
but lest we forget,
to salute our regret,
so our hearts won't feel ashamed.

Morals take a slippery slope,
poppies make more profit as dope,
selling our sons
for the price of more guns
to claim we are remembering hope.

Banshee

Growling sky forewarns,
banshees screaming their attack,
red eyes weeping fire,
buildings stand like grim gallows,
smouldering from last night's flames.

Honour Them

Honour them,
fallen only to promise
others may stand
in their place thereafter,
holding up the Standard
celebrating victory,
captured and cheered,
enemy sneered,
smeared with defeat.

Each loss always
another's gain,
one man's son taken
is another son
of mankind
mistaken for the enemy
of humanity.

Weapons

Weapons empower
lonely, drunken, foolish minds,
drowned in bitter pride.

Soldier's Eulogy

He was an awful young man
with no sensible plan,
a nuisance from the day he was born.

The dirty bully was vagrant,
unpleasantly fragrant,
a scoundrel worth nothing but scorn.

He was a bastard like no other,
from a whore of a mother,
rotten right down to the core.

At least now he's gone
I'm not the only one
glad he's a burden no more.

This truth must be spoken,
the spell can be broken,
we will speak ill of the dead.

Let's make no pretence,
or give false defence,
for a life we just wasted instead.

Seasons of War

Salty beads roll down
my barren landscape;
scorched, congealed craters
divide the surface,
blazed with rays and fire,
consumed by draught
as all life curls contorted
back into dust.

Until skies open,
torrential flooding,
mud-glue fills every valley,
collapsing into sodden
soaked relapsing
falling life trudging
knee-high in struggle
desperate to escape.

Solid numbness,
pierced with jagged ice,
searing pain slicing
the sight-snatched squinted eyes,
blinded, blizzard-frozen,
defences ceasing and failing
on rock-earth,
as long nights darken hope.

Green air lingers,
tempting fresh resolve,

new light offers promise
that Mother might blossom bless,
on the few fingers which remain,
deftly sprinkling seeds of life
from her bosom which one day
promised peace for us all.

Valentine for Dresden

Roses are red
violence is blue
love keeps forgetting
how we murdered you.

Chance of War

Blood-stained deck of cards
cut and held towards the heart,
turned on cries of war.

Peace

Resist winning urge;
Inspire joy in salvation;
Prosper in shared peace.

Shell Shock

Bang.
All day long.
Bang.
My rifle up against my head.
Bang. Bang.
I'll shoot bang and shoot bang
until he's dead.
Bang.
Blistering whistles fill the air,
land with a bang.
Blood sprays across my face,
bang limbs fly,
smells of burning, bang
eyes fill with human soot
bang I can feel
death underfoot,
commands screamed out,
bang, bang,
I cannot bang hear,
which way should I turn,
bang flash bang bright bang burn,
fumble at my rifle,
bang fingers numb,
head squeezing,
bang captured,
drag-kick-writhe-mad,
too many hands,
slam me inside,

bang shuts the cold steel door,
darkness roars,
rattle bang.
Bang.
Bang.
Then:
nothing,
but thumping
in my chest,
pounding
in my head.

PTSD

Peace-time suffering demons,
Tormented, dark, petrified screams,
Soul performs tortured depravity,
Disappearing serves tyrant's profit.

War Blunder

Blunder the thunder,
lighting-strike innocent souls,
out-storming freedom.

Who am I now?

Who am I now?
Who am I?
All I see,
hatred in those eyes,
dried from all the cries,
hidden by His lies,
that I fight
for good so common
yet known by few.

What am I now?
What am I?
A mere part,
metal to the ground,
trapped inside these bounds
hidden by the sounds,
that I fear
like sleepless nights
eased on by few.

Where am I now?
Where am I?
All I smell,
embers of my soul
burned inside this hole,
hell-bound by my role,
'til I fall
with blackened-dead heart
held warm by few.
Who am I now,
but a shadow of you?

Debt Across the Ages

If tears come so easy
for those that we've lost,
why did they run before
we sacrificed the cost?

We spent our fallen fortunes,
ripped all love apart,
like flesh between our teeth,
calling war an art.

Brush filled with blood
stroking muddied pages,
till regret consumes excuses
growing debt across the ages.

Means & Ends

Fighting for an end,
presumed honour in service,
bears no worthy means.

The Last Refuge

In whatever name you stand,
wearing whichever cloth,
or skin,
faith or family,
even alone,
do so in honour.
Hold your head high
so even the fallen shall live
in memory of what they gave
to see humanity saved.
Just as Pandora,
you released
depravity and disease,
of mind and body,
living hell on earth,
death of all mirth,
betrayal of innocence,
our weakest
never deserved,
she preserved
the last refuge:
hope.

Sky Beasts

Sky beasts hunt weak prey
dropping their screeching thunder,
feasting on burnt hope.

Sniper

Raises his arm peacefully,
graceful to the lips,
bitter flavour familiar,
closes his eyes.
Inhales.

Holds a moment of pleasure,
soothed by warm poison,
relaxed by habit,
moment released
from tense reservation.
Exhales.

Blue-grey plume appears,
freezing on cold air,
slowly dancing away
on a light breeze.
Chewing ice,
I watch the plume,
but without setting chase.
Inhale. Exhale.
Squeeze.

Final Moment

We stand together
worlds apart
fighting a battle
we did not start:

we share
this brutal final moment
we stare
this brutal final moment.

We wait together
worlds apart
ready to die
for Ares' art:

we share
this brutal final moment
we stare
this brutal final moment.

We shall bleed together
worlds apart
our final breath
for a frozen heart:

we share
this brutal final moment
we stare
this brutal final moment.

We fail together
worlds apart
silent trigger
faulted start:
we share
this brutal final moment
we stare
this brutal final moment.

We charge together
worlds apart
losing a war
we did not start:

we share
this brutal final moment
we stare
this brutal final moment.

In this brutal final moment
our worlds collide,
we fall together,
bleed together,
die together.

Perhaps we might have shared
more than a knife
if fate had cared
for life.

Soldier's Goodbye

Silk hands caress my cheeks,
thumbs gently catch the tears,
fingers comb through my hair
and dance it to perfection
only a mother can see.

As we brave our meeting gaze,
deep in glistening eyes,
I see the storm in your soul:
gales of pride battling
thunders of fear.

Your smile quivers,
lower lip hides its shiver,
plump rosy peach-skin chin,
gently rippling,
holding back your heart's thoughts.

Warm palm softens my nape
as you fondly recall
memories of childhood,
mischiefs of adolescence,
mortality of maturity.

Your gentle whispers
fall soft as cherry blossom,
filled with fragrant hope
of maternal promise
in my infant ears.

And as we release,
torn by time and fate,
you sigh: "I love you,"
raising a finger to my lips,
silencing my soldier's goodbye.

Shell

Here I lie on bloodied ground,
terrifying power and hideous sound,
purposed only to steal or destroy,
the lives and futures from our boys,
pretending murder made them free,
playing games no-one's eyes should see,
learning to lose when most succeeding,
yearning to win when all is left bleeding.

Pitched towards the blackened sky,
called to duty by a callous cry,
dance performed, brothers turn their backs,
my smooth coat loaded with jagged attack,
Reeper's scythe swings my deadly arc,
splinters fill the petrified dark,
consuming flesh and splitting bone,
only by silence are the dead ever known.

Dresden's Valentine

Hearts were bloodied, buried and burned
one vicious eve of Valentine,
crushed into rubble, ashes upturned,
not long after clocks struck nine.

Lights descended like Christmas trees
to whip up the night-time skies,
guiding down the two-ton cookies
gorging on innocent cries.

Flaming-fists of waves all broke,
more tidal than the last;
horizon blackened with acrid smoke,
blinding with every blast.

No fathers, mothers, children spared,
their prayers were all too late,
for all the love that Dresden dared
was met with Hades' hate.

Last Supper

Last supper rains down
bitter metal taste lingers
vengeance served with blood.

Birds of Britain

Wings spread wide,
arms in the air
conquering the slide.
We're up there with you,
by your side,
swooping belly
up with pride
to force back
the blackened tide,
parting its wave
in heroic collide,
daring the dodgems
and roller-coaster ride

to free us
from the darkness
where we must hide.

Hold our hearts high
as you soar the skies:
birds of Britain.

Pride in War

Makes men out of boys;
Morphs monsters out of good men;
Mocks peace with its pride.

My Duty

I take out my pistol
fire shots with one hand
hit him in the chest
his mother will understand
it was my duty.

I shoulder my rifle
fire rounds with both hands
they fall in their numbers
their mothers will understand
it was my duty.

I load another mortar
fired high above the land
spread limbs across fields
all their mothers will understand
it was my duty.

I aim the tonnes of turret
blast craters in the land
obliterate faceless enemies
every mother will understand
it was my duty.

I check numbers off lists
ordering as planned
packing onto trains
accompanying mothers understand
it is my duty.

I keep it in the line
place soap in its hand
shut the door behind
I know God understands:
it was just my duty.

Blackened

Stood on top of the Thames,
wondering at fairy-lights,
softly shimmering peace,
warming the city to sleep.
Little eyes softly close,
one by one,
as night whispers in.

But the darkness
drowns the magic,
swallowing the world
into a blackened
abyss of fear.
Monsters menace
midnight skies,
creeping,
threatening,
bringing the blaze
to burn the horizon.

Brave

I looked into her eyes
burnt red with grief
hoping words could summon
comfort
pride
relief,

sincere enough to hide
failure of humanity,
horror and betrayal
loss,
murder,
insanity.

Mother's greatest fear,
bloody blade of blame,
shell shock to her mind,
dishonour,
humiliation,
shame.

How could she survive,
forgive or forget
brutal judgement,
injustice,
anger,
regret?

I made a choice,
his memory I'd save,
my friend and comrade
died
dutiful,
brave.

Secret Books of Auschwitz

Children gathered under false pretence,
permission granted only to provide
punishment and persecution
of elder branded slaves,
already doomed to rocky graves,
their purpose exhausted,
stacked en masse as bones
stolen from life and death.

But a small library of books,
collection cobbled for little eyes
as a haven hidden from hell,
forbidden enjoyment and smiles,
smited by hatred,
wrapped their lips
around the secret song of words
shielded by love and innocence.

Little lives escaped in art;
their guardian gifted freedom.

Forgive

Forgive.
If not for our heroes,
we have a future free,
saved by imprisonment,
depraved choices made
by a decorated few
adorned by their success
of pure bloody evil
spent against innocence.

Should we ever forgive?
Sleepless nights spent wondering
if those men with bony arms,
purposed merely to survive,
exist against extinction
fuelled by spite,
cursed with hatred,
fought with every poisoned gasp,
petrified by terror-clasp,
strangled to the last
stolen thoughts,
would have forgiven?

How can we ever forgive,
if we claim to never forget,
acting as if
we are too poor in regret
to stop repeating
our crimes
for the sake
of the comfort
of the few?

Bullet

Hiding in my shell,
pregnant with unborn power,
I live to bring death.

Wealth

Flesh burns acrid smoke,
bones shatter beyond repair,
yet wealth still survives.

Ceasefire

Taut-minded bloodthirst,
engines smog trigger-poised air:
call the silence 'peace.'

Mr Anderson

Dear Mr Anderson
I hate for me an' me sis to be a pain

but can we hide under your tortoise shell,
'cause the crows are dropping stones again,

there's that sicky gassy smell,
our roof's all broken an' lets in the rain,

all the walls are cracked and fell,
an' now sis has started a cryin' campaign,

Grandpa's shouting like he's seen hell,
Ma says he's got a broken brain,

Grandma's still in bed unwell,
Daddy didn't come back on the train.

We tried next door,
rang the bell,
no-one answered,
or heard,
maybe they are
in their own...?

Please, Mr Anderson,
we'd ask around
but everyone's
gone.

A Letter Home

Dear Mother,
I write to say
I killed a little boy today.

He held no weapon,
posed no threat,
wore a smile
I'll never forget:
he quivered with uncertain
shivering eyes,
delicious with hope,
sharing a forbidden moment
with mine.

Dishevelled innocence,
his delicate hand held out,
showed me a red ball,
limped a step my way,
dragging his striped
sack of bones,
yearning
for me to play
a different game today,
more fun than hiding,
waiting like stone.

He pained one pace closer,
filled with naïve desire.

A dark shadow loomed,
like claws
on walls
of the night-time bedroom,
drew my eye,
as it approached.

Taller, wider
contorted talons
growing upside down,
pulsing a commanding gait,
decorated with blackened steel,
prowling, hunting,
weapon poised.

His hooks bit
into the boy's shoulder,
like the vampire
gorging his thirst from youth
as he hissed loud enough
for my trained ear:
"Wo ist er?"

Fear
stole the boy's voice
as the shadow landed
on both shoulders,
craning its neck,
spying down the boy's arm,
seeking its prey.

"Zeige auf ihn,"
hissed so hot,
burning the babe's flesh,
tears rushed to cool
from eyes that fixed
on me.
"Komm heraus"
bellowed the beast,
biting at the boy's ear.

I could not move
for fight nor flight,
duty nor fear,
trapped by the tormenter,
who stood again,
proud with intention
and menace.

One swift move,
side-arm stabbed
like a needle
to the tender temple.
"Komm heraus, oder ich schiesse den Jungen."

Silence.
Stillness,
until quakes engulfed the child,
tell-tale tide
bled from his groin,
upturned smile contorted his soul.

I felt the shockwave.
I felt the red ball bounce.
I felt his body fall
like skittles
in a striped sack
sealed with yellow insignia.

The shadow fixed a glare
my way,
waiting for
my move,
daring for
my anger,
goading for
my vengeance,
wiped its weapon,
red handkerchief
branded with hate.
All the time glaring.
Smiling.
He nodded
as he raised his killing wing
and saluted me,
"Gut gespielt."
swooped away.

Numb.
All humanity
dead and drained,
my blood frozen
in shame.

Dear Mother,
I write to say
I killed a little boy today.
He held no weapon,
posed no threat,
wore a smile
I'll never forget.

Acknowledgements

Special thanks to *Patricia M Osborne* for her wisdom and generosity in editing the collection. An author and poet in her own right, her support, creativity and guidance are always a valuable part of fine-tuning my poetry.

I am also privileged to have an original *Rob Parkinson* painting as the cover art of the book. Working with him to capture the spirit of this collection in visual form was a pleasure. Rob's artwork is as moving as it is beautiful, and I'm proud to invite readers to judge my book by its cover.

Other Works by the Author

Poetry
Ripples

Novels & Short Stories
To Die For
Stench of Death & Mulch

Plays
No Smoke

Find out more about the writer on his website

www.inasmanywords.com

and on social media as

@inasmanywords
&
@colinwardwriter

www.ingramcontent.com/pod-product-compliance
Lightning Source LLC
Chambersburg PA
CBHW020546130626
46552CB00007B/2771